Whee-e-e,
What a Ride!

Happy Birthday,
Daisy!

Playtime
at Preschool!

Produced by Kroha Associates, Inc.
Middletown, Connecticut.
Illustrated by Alvin S. White Studio
Burbank, California.
Printed in the United States of America.
ISBN 1-56326-009-3

Today the Disney Babies learned something new at preschool. Their teacher taught them the names of some shapes. Then it was play time. "Let's play blocks!" said Baby Donald.

"Look! A triangle," said Baby Mickey,
reaching for a green block. Baby Goofy picked
up some red blocks and asked, "What's this
shape? I forgot." Donald bragged, "I know!
They're rectangles."

"Hey!" cried Goofy. "Here are some more . . . umm, tr-tr . . ." Goofy tried to remember the name of the green shapes. "Tree-angles?" he asked.

"Not tree-angles, Goofy. They're triangles," corrected Mickey.

"Who cares about shapes?" said Baby Pete. "I want these blocks. They're the biggest!" And Pete carried away all the big yellow blocks.

While Pete played in a corner by himself, the
other Disney Babies had a great idea.

"Let's make a big castle!" said Donald.

"We can put all our blocks together," added
Goofy.

"Not me," called Pete. "These big blocks are
mine!"

"But, Pete! We need those," objected
Mickey.

"Aww, come on, Pete," pleaded Goofy.
"Give me one big block."
"No! I need them all," insisted Pete.

Goofy wanted a big yellow block so much.
He set down a green block by Pete and said,
"Let's trade! I'll give you this . . . please?
Please ?"

"No. I'm keeping my blocks!" said Pete.

"Come on, Goofy," called Mickey. "We don't need those blocks. Let's start a big castle!"

Goofy grinned and said, "Wait for me!"

"Big castle, hah!" thought Pete. "Not with those little blocks!" He watched his friends stack one block on top of another.

"Humph," he thought. "That looks easy. I'll make a bigger castle."

"Hey, watch me!" Pete yelled. He tried to
stack the blocks. "This'll be huge!" But BONK!
BOOM! Pete's blocks tumbled to the floor.

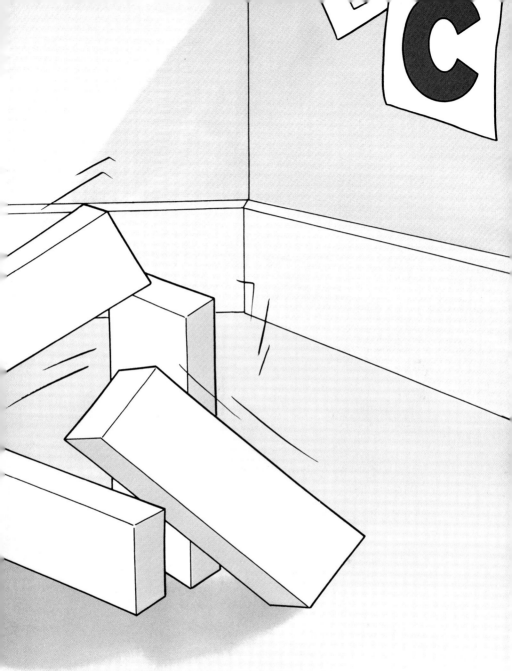

Pete started over and carefully stacked up
the blocks. But soon his tower began to shake.
"No! Don't fall!" he shouted. CRASH! The
blocks fell again!

Mickey, Goofy, and Donald had used most of
their blocks on the castle. Still, something looked
wrong.

"It's not big enough yet," said Donald.

"We need big blocks for the roof," said Mickey.

"Goofy, go tell Pete," urged Donald.
"Oh, no! Not me again!" groaned Goofy.
"You ask him."

Everyone had a problem! Pete's big blocks kept falling down, and the other Disney Babies needed Pete's blocks to finish their castle.

"This is no fun!" Pete pouted. He liked his friends' castle because it didn't fall down. "Maybe they'll let me play, too," he thought.

Pete carried his blocks over to the castle and said, "Hey, everybody, try this!" He put a big block on top of the castle to see how the others liked it.

"Yes!" shouted Mickey. "More yellow blocks, Pete!"

"Time for another tr-tr-triangle!" said Goofy, proud that he had remembered the name of the shape.

"I still like the big blocks best," said Pete.

Donald had found some flags by the toy box, and he was saving them as a surprise.

"Look at these!" he announced, waving the bright red flags.

Mickey put the last flag on the castle.
"Hooray! It's finished!" shouted Donald, as
they sat back to admire their work.

"A castle needs lots of different blocks," said Mickey.

"And lots of different friends!" added Pete with a grin. He had just decided that playing alone with the biggest blocks wasn't nearly as much fun as playing with friends!

Parenting Matters

Dear Parent,

Learning to get along with others and to share things, such as blocks and toys, is a challenge for children. At first, young children play alone, but as they develop and participate in social situations such as preschool, they learn to play with others. Games and projects that require a group effort teach children the value of teamwork and cooperation, both of which are important to success later in life.

In *They're My Blocks!* Baby Pete discovers that sharing his big yellow blocks with the other Disney Babies is more fun than hoarding them and playing by himself. After Pete contributes his much-needed blocks to the building of a giant castle and joins in the team effort, he learns that cooperating with others is rewarding and enjoyable.

They're My Blocks! helps young children learn that:

* activities are more fun when children cooperate with others and work together.
* sharing with others is an important and necessary part of growing up.
* being part of a group effort is something to be proud of.

Some Hints for Parents

* Show children how to play games that teach teamwork, such as tug-of-war, and activities that encourage cooperation, such as hide-and-seek and block-building.
* Encourage children to share toys with visitors or siblings, and help children take turns choosing which games to play or which stories to read first, so everyone can be a winner.
* When children find it hard to share, show them that you understand their feelings and their friends' feelings, then offer a compromise.